W9-AKB-398

Kevin

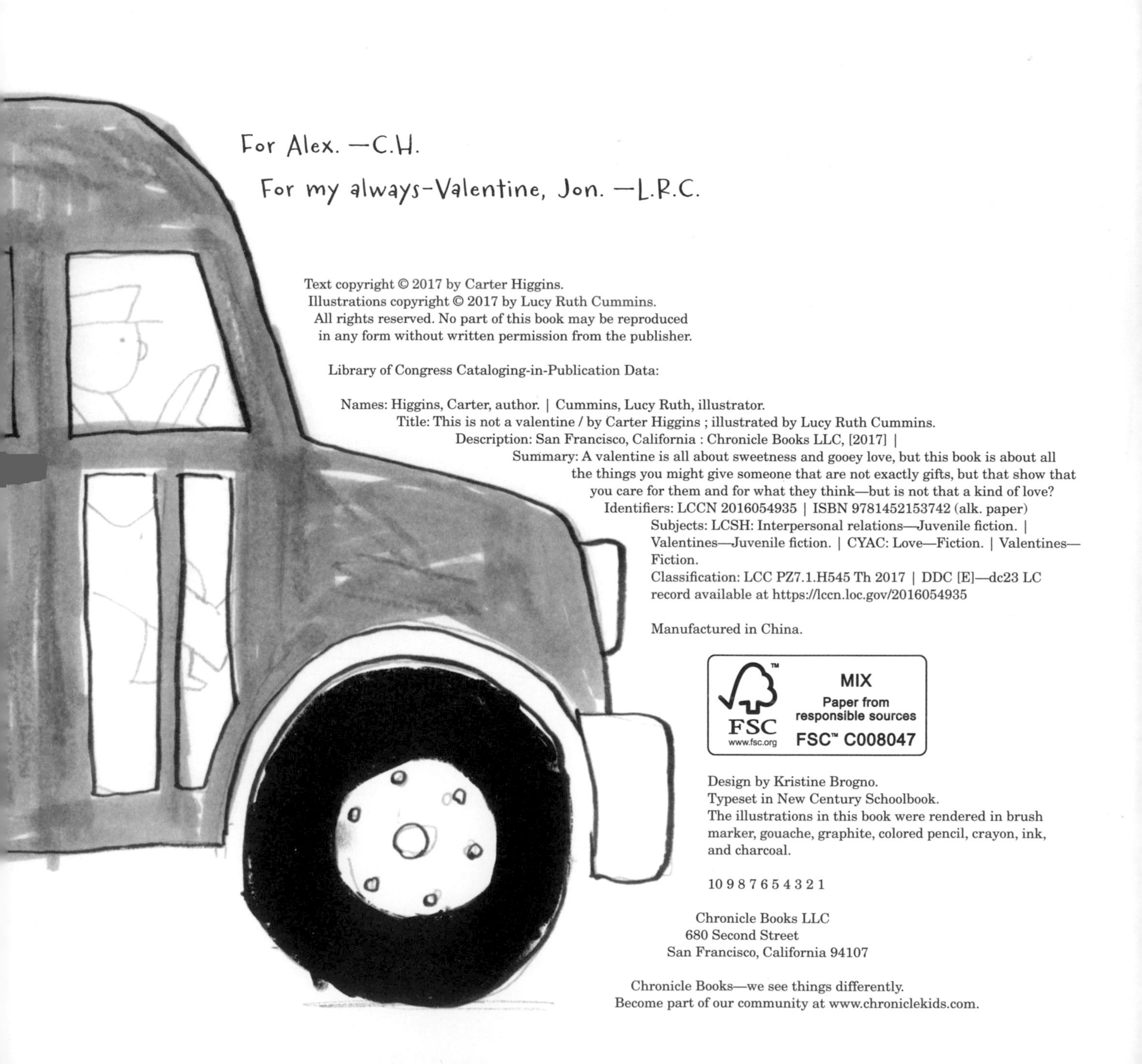

For Alex. —C.H.

For my always-Valentine, Jon. —L.R.C.



Library of Congress Cataloging-in-Publication Data:

Names: Higgins, Carter, author. | Cummins, Lucy Ruth, illustrator.
Title: This is not a valentine / by Carter Higgins ; illustrated by Lucy Ruth Cummins.
Description: San Francisco, California : Chronicle Books LLC, [2017] |
Summary: A valentine is all about sweetness and gooey love, but this book is about all the things you might give someone that are not exactly gifts, but that show that you care for them and for what they think—but is not that a kind of love?
Identifiers: LCCN 2016054935 | ISBN 9781452153742 (alk. paper)
Subjects: LCSH: Interpersonal relations—Juvenile fiction. | Valentines—Juvenile fiction. | CYAC: Love—Fiction. | Valentines—Fiction.
Classification: LCC PZ7.1.H545 Th 2017 | DDC [E]—dc23 LC record available at https://lccn.loc.gov/2016054935

Manufactured in China.

FSC www.fsc.org MIX Paper from responsible sources FSC™ C008047

Design by Kristine Brogno.
Typeset in New Century Schoolbook.
The illustrations in this book were rendered in brush marker, gouache, graphite, colored pencil, crayon, ink, and charcoal.

10 9 8 7 6 5 4 3 2 1

Chronicle Books LLC
680 Second Street
San Francisco, California 94107

Chronicle Books—we see things differently.
Become part of our community at www.chroniclekids.com.

# This Is NOT a Valentine

Written by Carter Higgins * Illustrated by Lucy Ruth Cummins

chronicle books san francisco

STOP

This is not a valentine,

since those come with buckets of roses
and bushels of tulips
that smell like grannies
fresh out of the garden.

All I’ve got are these
and I already blew the wishes
off most of them, for a rocket ship
or the last cinnamon bun
or moon boots and a mega-blaster.

This is not a valentine,

since jewels and gems belong in treasure chests
or museums or on ladies who sing at the opera.

And the fanciest ones don't come out of
some machine at a grocery store anyway.
But this one matches your best shoelaces.
If it won't get past your knuckles
you could wear it on a string.

This is <u>not</u> a valentine,

since sparkle and pink and glitter are not your favorite colors.

You like the brown in the mud puddle
and fish-food orange
and that purpley-blue on your nose
when it's a mittens kind of day.
But red is pretty good for superheroes,
and you are my favorite one.

This is not a valentine,

since those things have
fancy cursive and swoopy spins
on words that sound like mush.

This one is scraps and rips
and drippy glue that dried funny
and the green marker was the
only one that worked.

Besides,
the teacher
made us
make these.

This is *not*
a valentine,

since you're up there at the front of the line and I am the caboose.

Maybe one day
we'll both
be in the middle.
I hope it's a Wednesday.
Maybe a Monday.
Or any of those other days, really.
Until then, this *w h o o s h* .

FRIDAY
HURSDAY
28
27
19
MONDAY
SUNDAY
23
22
17

This is <u>not</u> a valentine,

since the cooties tumble out when you open one of those.

But if you get the cooties
and I get the cooties,
then we can have cherry juice
and chicken soup with rice
together.

This is not a valentine,

since sugared hearts and suckers
give you cavities and bellyaches.

But I found this at the bottom
of my lunchbox.
You can have the jelly side,
cause I like peanut butter best.
Maybe I'll have some left over.
Maybe.

This is not
a valentine,

since it’s got
sharper edges than
dainty old lace.

But if you play duck duck goose
with kids who run real fast,
you'll just get stuck in the stew pot.
So meet me at the hopscotch squares.
My lucky rock will help.

This is *not*
a valentine,

since it’s not giggles and
whispers about where
the best hiding spots are.

(But the second-best one is
in the hollow of that trunk.
That one,
over there.
We're the only ones who know.)

This is not a valentine,

since I don’t only like you today.
I like you tomorrow and next Tuesday
and last week, too.

I like you all the days

the school bell rings

just
one more
time.

Alex
Edward
Julie
Elizabeth
Hannah
Oli
Rubin
Jon
Snow
Roman
Emily
Nate
Luca